For my parents

Thank you: Tom Gauld, Sarah Gonzales, Judy Hansen,
Mina Ino, Izumi Sakamoto, Cole Sanchez, Paula Wiseman,
and Soy Sauce Bookstore in Kofu, Japan.

SIMON & SCHUSTER BOOKS FOR YOUNG READERS
An imprint of Simon & Schuster Children's Publishing Division
1230 Avenue of the Americas, New York, New York 10020
Copyright © 2019 by Matthew Forsythe

SIMON & SCHUSTER BOOKS FOR YOUNG READERS
is a trademark of Simon & Schuster, Inc.
For information about special discounts for bulk purchases, please contact Simon & Schuster
Special Sales at 1-866-506-1949 or business@simonandschuster.com.
The Simon & Schuster Speakers Bureau can bring authors to your live event.
For more information or to book an event, contact the Simon & Schuster Speakers Bureau
at 1-866-248-3049 or visit our website at www.simonspeakers.com.
Book design by Jonathan Yamakami
The text for this book was set in Goudy Modern MT Std.
The illustrations for this book were rendered in watercolor, gouache, and colored pencil.
Manufactured in China
0719 SCP
First Edition
2 4 6 8 10 9 7 5 3 1
Library of Congress Cataloging-in-Publication Data
Names: Forsythe, Matthew, 1976– author, illustrator.
Title: Pokko and the drum / Matthew Forsythe.
Description: First edition. | New York : Simon & Schuster Books for Young Readers, [2019] |
"A Paula Wiseman Book." | Summary: When Pokko plays her drum in the forest she suddenly
finds herself surrounded by an entire band of animal musicians.
Identifiers: LCCN 2019000338|
ISBN 9781481480390 (hardcover) | ISBN 9781481480406 (eBook)
Subjects: | CYAC: Forest animals—Fiction. | Musicians—Fiction. | Drum—Fiction.
Classification: LCC PZ7.1.F663 Po 2019 | DDC [E]—dc23
LC record available at https://lccn.loc.gov/2019000338

POKKO
AND THE
DRUM

MATTHEW FORSYTHE

A Paula Wiseman Book
Simon & Schuster Books for Young Readers
New York   London   Toronto   Sydney   New Delhi

The biggest mistake Pokko's parents ever made was giving her a drum.

They had made mistakes before.

Like the slingshot.

And the llama.

And the balloon.

But the drum was the biggest mistake.

"We shouldn't have given her that drum,"
said her father.

"What?" said her mother.
"The drum is too loud, I can't hear you."

"The drum was a big mistake,"
said her father.

"That sounds like a wonderful idea,"
said her mother, who still couldn't hear
what he was saying.

The next day her father said,
"Pokko, why don't you take your
drum outside for a little while.

"But don't make too much noise.
We're just a little frog family
that lives in a mushroom, and
we don't like drawing attention
to ourselves."

Pokko agreed.

And she set out as quietly
as she could.

It had just rained, and the forest
was sparkling like an emerald.

And it was very quiet.

Too quiet.

Pokko started tapping on her drum just to keep herself company.

But something stirred behind her.

A raccoon playing a banjo started following her.

So Pokko hit her drum louder.

And then a rabbit
playing a trumpet
started following
them.

But Pokko kept
playing her drum.

And then a wolf—who couldn't really play anything
but was very happy to be near the music—joined in.

And Pokko still played her drum.

But then the wolf ate the rabbit, and Pokko stopped
playing her drum and faced the wolf and said,

"No more eating band members
or you're out of the band."

"I'm sorry," said the wolf,

and he meant it.

And then they all started playing again, and soon there was a crowd of animals playing instruments . . .

and a crowd of animals following them
around enjoying the music.

And they were all following Pokko.

"Pokko, your dinner is ready!"
shouted her father.

No one answered, but he could hear
music in the distance.

And the music grew louder.

And louder.

Until the crowd swept through the house
and carried Pokko's parents off into the woods.

"Oh, no!" said her father.
"Oh, dear!" said her mother.

"I think that's Pokko down in front!"
said her father. "And you know what?"

"What?" said her mother, who was just getting to the best part of her book.

"I think she's pretty good!"

And no one could hear what he was saying,
but if they could . . .

they all would have agreed.